Welcome to Percy's Park!

Percy the park keeper
works hard looking after
the park and his animal
friends who live there.
But Percy still likes to
find time for some fun
and games. And, of
course, in Percy's Park,
there's always time
for a story…

After The Storm

First published in hardback in Great Britain by HarperCollins Publishers Ltd in 1992
First published in paperback by Picture Lions in 1993
New edition published by Collins Picture Books in 2003
This edition published by HarperCollins Children's Books in 2011

13 15 17 19 20 18 16 14 12

ISBN: 978-0-00-715515-6

Picture Lions and Collins Picture Books are imprints of the Children's Division,
part of HarperCollins Publishers Ltd.
HarperCollins Children's Books is a division of HarperCollins Publishers Ltd.

Text and illustrations copyright © Nick Butterworth 1992, 2011

Visit our website at: www.harpercollins.co.uk

Printed in China

Nick Butterworth

After The Storm

HarperCollins *Children's Books*

Percy the park keeper couldn't sleep.
Outside his hut a great storm was raging,
with thunder and lightning and pouring rain.

Percy wasn't frightened by the thunder and he
loved to watch the lightning as it lit up the whole
park. He didn't even mind the rain.

But there was one thing that Percy didn't like.

He didn't like the wind. It blew down fences in the park and ripped branches off the trees. He didn't like it one bit.

"Oh dear," he sighed as he watched from his window. The wind tugged at the trees, making them creak and groan. "It looks like I'm going to be busy tomorrow."

He pulled his pillow over his head and tried to get to sleep.

Percy was up early in the morning. The wind had stopped and the sky was clear.

Percy loaded up his wheelbarrow with all the things he would need to make repairs and clear up after the storm. Then he set off to inspect the damage.

He felt happy as he took deep breaths of the fresh, clean air. Perhaps the damage wouldn't be too bad.

But he was wrong. Something dreadful had happened. A great big oak tree that had stood by itself on top of a little hill had been blown over by the storm.

The giant tree had been one of Percy's favourites. Now it looked very sad lying on its side with its mass of tangly roots sticking up into the air.

But it wasn't just one of Percy's favourite trees; some of Percy's animal friends lived there. Now their homes were wrecked.

Percy hurried up to the fallen tree.

The animals were gathered by the tree looking cross and unhappy. When they saw Percy everyone started talking at once.

P ercy sat down with his friends and listened as they told how the storm had brought down the great tree.

"And now we have nowhere to live," said the badger. "Some of us lived in the tree and some of us lived under it. But we're all homeless now."

Some of the rabbits looked close to tears and the fox was very sniffy. Percy passed him his handkerchief and the fox blew his nose.

Percy stood up.

"We'll just have to find you somewhere else to live," he said. "Come on everybody. Jump into my wheelbarrow." The animals felt better now that Percy was with them.

First he took them to the pine wood. But nobody wanted to live there.

"Too dark," squeaked the mice.

"Too gloomy," said the hedgehog.

So Percy took them to the shrubbery. But nobody wanted to live in the shrubbery either.

"No big trees," complained the squirrels.

"No big roots," moaned the rabbits.

"Never mind," said Percy. "We'll try across the stream."

Percy began to push the heavy wheelbarrow over a little bridge that crossed the stream. But as he got to the middle of the bridge, two things happened.

Percy stumbled. And the wheelbarrow decided to see what it would be like to be a boat. SP-LASH!

Suddenly Percy and his friends found themselves drifting downstream to where the stream opened out into a lake.

Percy stood up and looked around.

"We'll have to paddle back to the shore," he said. But then something caught his eye.

"No, wait," said Percy. "Let's paddle across to the other side of the lake. I have an idea."

The animals looked puzzled. What was Percy up to? Slowly they paddled the wheelbarrow across the lake.

"Here we are!" said Percy. The squirrels jumped ashore and tied up the wheelbarrow to the roots of an enormous hollow tree that grew by the water's edge.

"Now this is my plan," said Percy. Everyone gathered round as Percy explained his idea.

"Is everybody clear?" Everyone nodded.

"Then let's get to work!"

They began by unloading all Percy's tools and the planks of wood from the wheelbarrow. Then Percy explained exactly what he wanted each one to do.

He showed the badger how to use a saw and he showed the squirrels how to knock in nails. The fox drilled holes and the rabbits screwed in screws. The mice were kept busy fetching and carrying for everyone else.

At lunchtime they took a short break to share some of Percy's peanut butter sandwiches. Then they got busy again.

At long last their work was finished. A very tired Percy stood back to admire their handiwork.

Now the squirrels had a brand new home…

and so did the mice.

The rabbits had a new home…

and so did the badger.

And the fox.

And the hedgehog.

In fact, every one of Percy's
friends had a fine new place to live.

"Well done everybody!" said Percy. "This is the best tree house I've ever seen!"

"What about you Percy?" called the badger. "Aren't you going to join us?"

Percy smiled.

"I think I'll stick to my old hut," he said.

"Besides," said Percy, taking an acorn out of his pocket, "I still have one job left to do back at the little hill!"

"I was born in London in 1946 and grew up in a sweet shop in Essex. For several years I worked as a graphic designer, but in 1980 I decided to concentrate on writing and illustrating books for children.

My wife, Annette, and I have two grown-up children, Ben and Amanda, and we have put down roots in the country.

I haven't recently counted how many books there are with my name on the cover but Percy the Park Keeper accounts for a good many of them. I'm reliably informed that they have sold in their millions, worldwide. Hooray!

I didn't realise this when I invented Percy, but I can now see that he's very like my mum's dad, my grandpa. Here's a picture of him giving a ride to my mum and my brother, Mike, in his old home-made wheelbarrow!"

Nick Butterworth

Nick Butterworth has presented children's stories on television, worked on a strip for *Sunday Express Magazine* and worked for various major graphic design companies. Among his books published by HarperCollins are *Thud!*, *QPootle5*, *Jingle Bells*, *Albert le Blanc*, *Tiger* and *The Whisperer*, which won the Nestlé Gold Award. But he is best-known for his stories about Percy the Park Keeper. There are now more than 30 books about Percy, who features on audio CD and DVD, as well as having appeared in his own television series.

Collect all the Percy the Park Keeper stories
OVER 7 MILLION BOOKS SOLD!

PB: 978-0-00-714693-2

PB: 978-0-00-715515-6

PB: 978-0-00-715516-3

PB: 978-0-00-715518-7

PB: 978-0-00-715517-0

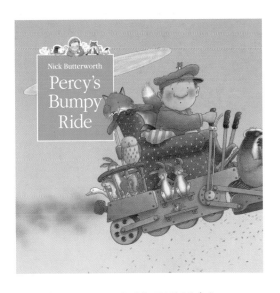

PB: 978-0-00-715514-9

Percy the Park Keeper stories can be ordered at:

www.harpercollins.co.uk